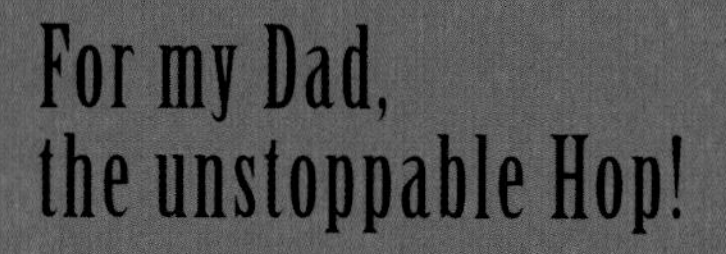

For my Dad,
the unstoppable Hop!

And for everyone who has
ever looked up at the
stars and wondered,
is there anybody out there?

With thanks to
Emily Ford
Kayt Bochenski
Chris Inns
and Gill Gribbin

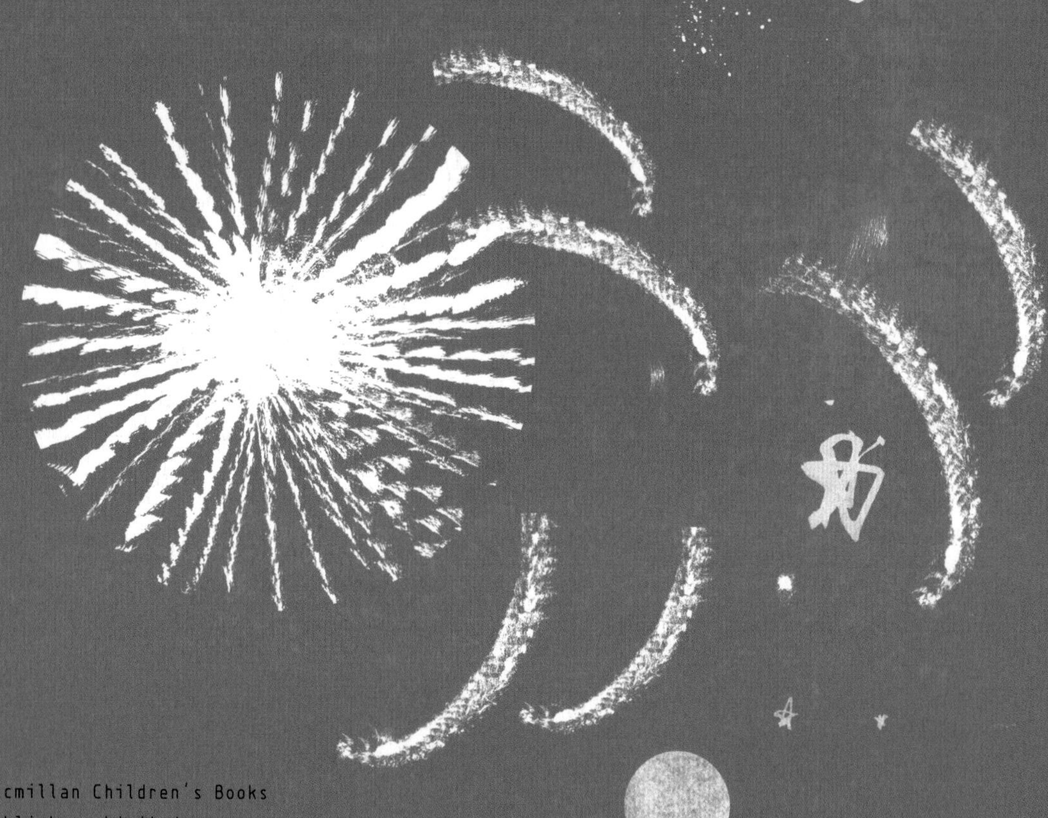

First published 2011 by Macmillan Children's Books
a division of Macmillan Publishers Limited
20 New Wharf Road, London N1 9RR
Basingstoke and Oxford
Associated companies throughout the world
www.panmacmillan.com

ISBN: 978-0-230-74816-3

1 3 5 7 9 8 6 4 2

A CIP catalogue record for this book is available from the British Library.

Printed in Belgium

UnpOppable

timhopgood

MACMILLAN CHILDREN'S BOOKS

"It's unpOppable!" said the boy,

as he stood on his big yellow balloon.

"It's unpOppable!" **said the boy,**

as it blew into the holly tree.

"It's un**pOp**pable!" said the boy,

as it danced along the aerials.

"It's **unstOppable!"** said the boy,

as it drifted up above the chimneys.

“Come back!” called the boy.

"Please don't go!"

But the yellow balloon didn't seem to hear.

“My unpoppable, it’s disappeared,” sniffed the boy.

But the balloon knew

where it was going!

Up and up it went.

Higher than the stars, around the moon, and all the way past . . .

... the
Milky Way.

And still it didn't go pOp.

What's that?

Wondered the boy.

"Is this yours?"

said a strange voice

from behind the big balloon.

"Yes!" said the boy, **"it's my unpOppable!"**

"Well, thank you for sending it to find me,"

said the little spaceman.

"But this is no ordinary unpoppable"

"Are you

ready for

something

spectacular?"

pOp!

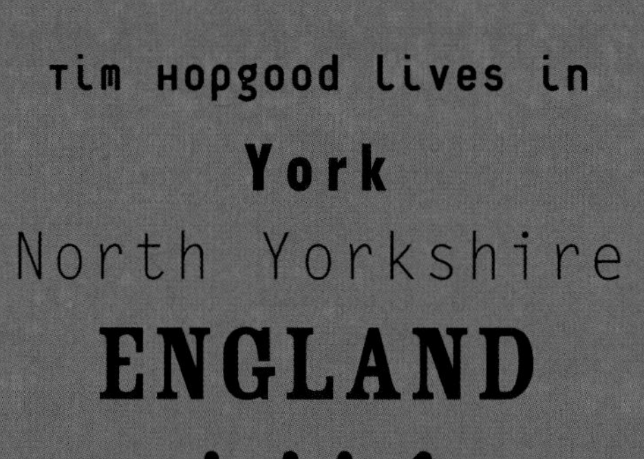

Tim Hopgood lives in

York

North Yorkshire

ENGLAND

UK

Europe

NORTHERN HEMISPHERE

PLANET EARTH

THE SOLAR SYSTEM

KUIPER BELT

Oort Cloud

Orion Spur

MILKY WAY GALAXY

THE DARK UNIVERSE

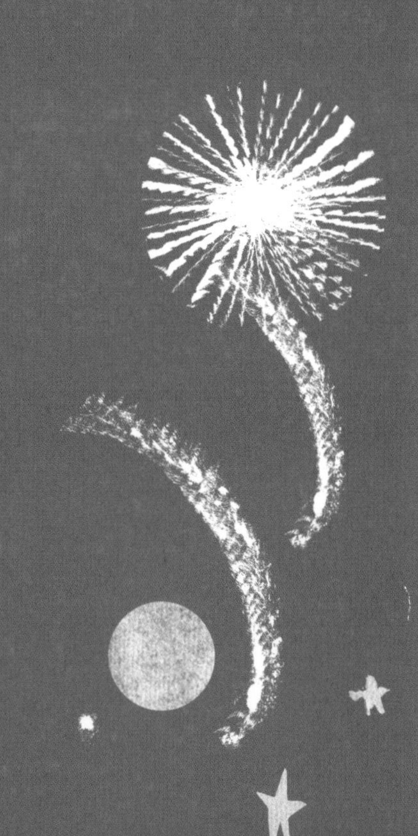